FROZEN II
MAGICAL STICKER BOOK

Penguin
Random
House

Written by Julia March and Lisa Stock
Project Editor: Lisa Stock
Senior Designer: Lynne Moulding

First American Edition, 2019
Published in the United States by DK Publishing
1745 Broadway, 20th Floor, New York NY 10019

Page design copyright © 2022 Dorling Kindersley Limited
DK, a Division of Penguin Random House LLC
24 25 15 14 13 12 11
012–311494–Oct/2019

A catalog record for this book is available from the Library of Congress.
ISBN: 978-1-4654-7902-0

DK books are available at special discounts when purchased in bulk for sales
promotions, premiums, fund-raising, or educational use.
For details, contact: DK Publishing Special Markets,
1745 Broadway, 20th Floor, New York NY 10019. SpecialSales@dk.com

Printed and bound in China

www.dk.com

How to use this book

**Read the captions,
then find the sticker that
best fits the space.**

(Hint: check the sticker labels for clues!)

**There are lots of fantastic
extra stickers, too!**

Secret whispers

In Arendelle, Queen Elsa rules wisely, surrounded by her loving sister and loyal friends. But something unsettling is happening. Elsa keeps hearing a strange voice calling her to leave her kingdom and travel north. What could the voice mean?

Elsa

Elsa cannot stop wondering where her magical powers come from. Nobody else in her family can create snow and ice!

Anna

Elsa's sister, Anna, just wants her family—and Arendelle—to be safe. But life does not always turn out how you want it to.

Kristoff

Kristoff is devoted to Anna and he wants to marry her. Now he just has to find the perfect moment to propose.

Sven

Even with Anna in his life, Kristoff still relies on his trusted reindeer pal. Some friendships don't need words!

Olaf

Now that Olaf can read, he is learning all he can about the world. The little snowman's sense of wonder grows and grows with every book he reads.

Charades

The group always makes time for family game night. They have fun together, even when Elsa's clues are a little... tricky.

Story time

As children, the princesses loved hearing the king and queen's tales of long ago. Their favorite was about an enchanted forest.

Sisterly bond

The sisters are very close. Anna can sense that something is bothering Elsa even before Elsa tells her about the voice.

To the north!

One night, the elements of nature suddenly leave Arendelle. Lights go out, water dries up, and a wind blows everyone out of their homes! Can the voice help Elsa undo this disaster? She follows it north to the Enchanted Forest. Inside, two old enemies—the Arendellians and the Northuldra—are trapped together.

Ice crystals

Elsa's magic turns the moisture in the sky into ice crystals. As they crash down, Arendelle is thrown into chaos.

Not alone

To the north lies the vast Enchanted Forest that Elsa must enter. She is glad her friends are coming with her!

Surrounded!

Charades

Water
Nokk

Sven

Anna

Grand Pabbie
Magical mist
The Dark Sea
Familiar face
Shipwreck
Floating off
Kristoff

Mattias

Honeymaren

Story time

Ice crystals

Elsa's journey

Wind Spirit

Earth Giants

Olaf

Ryder

Elsa

Special
scarf

Grand Pabbie
The troll Grand Pabbie explains to Elsa that her powers have awoken the spirits of the forest, and they are still angry.

Magical mist
A strange mist blocks the way into the forest. When Elsa holds onto Anna's hand, the mist magically parts to let the group inside.

Mattias
Lieutenant Mattias has been trapped in the Enchanted Forest for over 30 years. He is fiercely loyal to Arendelle.

Ryder Nattura
Ryder Nattura is Northuldra. He dreams of being set free from the Enchanted Forest. He has never set foot outside it.

Honeymaren
Ryder Nattura's sister is bold and brave. She doesn't see Elsa and Anna as enemies, but as possible keys to freedom.

Courage calls

Everyone will need courage to complete their missions. Elsa must trust the voice and go where it leads her—alone. Anna must learn to let go of people she loves. And all of them must strive to free the forest and turn foes into friends.

Surrounded!

The Northuldra and the Arendellians are still at odds after all these years. They can't even decide who will take the group as their prisoners!

Familiar face

Anna recognizes Mattias from somewhere. She realizes that she has seen his face in a portrait hanging in the palace!

Shipwreck

The voice leads Elsa and Anna to the wreck of an old ship. Its Arendellian flag identifies it as their parents' ship.

Floating off

Elsa is determined to face the dangerous Dark Sea alone. She creates an ice boat to send Anna and Olaf away from her and keep them safe.

The Dark Sea

Elsa dives into the Dark Sea. Maybe the answers she seeks are on the other side—where her parents' ship was headed.

Elsa's journey

Elsa's magical powers are hers alone. With great courage, she decides that she must finish her journey alone, too.

Elsa's message

Inside the cavern, Anna finds an icy message, sent from her sister across the Dark Sea. Suddenly, everything makes sense!

Spirits of nature

The nature spirits are the most mysterious dwellers in the Enchanted Forest. These magical beings can be dangerous! They may help or harm, depending on how much respect they are shown.

Earth Giants

The Earth Giants are huge, craggy spirits who shake the ground with every step. They could easily crush a person.

Special scarf

Elsa and Anna have a treasured scarf that belonged to their mother. Honeymaren explains how the symbols on it depict the forest spirits.

Wind Spirit

The Wind Spirit can be playful or destructive. When it mixes with Elsa's powers it can stir up a magical breeze.

Fire Spirit

Fire breaks out whenever this salamander is upset. He needs to calm down again in order to put out his flickering flames.

Water Nokk

This powerful Water Spirit takes the form of a large, prancing horse. He can only be ridden by those he deems worthy.